Please
Don't Tell Cooper
That Jack is a Rabbit

Michelle Lander Feinberg

Illustrations by

Anna Mosca

D1362429

Please Don't Tell Cooper That Jack is a Rabbit, Published September, 2021

Cover Design: Howard Johnson
Interior Design & Layout: Howard Johnson
Illustrations: Anna Mosca
Editorial & Proofreading: Highline Editorial, New York, NY, Karen Grennan

Photo credits: Author photo owned by Michelle Lander Feinberg

 SDP Publishing

Published by SDP Publishing, an imprint of SDP Publishing Solutions, LLC.
For more information about this book, contact Lisa Akoury-Ross at SDP Publishing by email at info@SDPPublishing.com.

To obtain permission(s) to use material from this work, please submit a written request to:

SDP Publishing
Permissions Department
PO Box 26
East Bridgewater, MA 02333
or email your request to info@SDPPublishing.com

ISBN-13 (paperback): 978-1-7361990-3-9
ISBN-13 (hardcover): 978-1-7367204-2-4
ISBN-13 (ebook): 978-1-7361990-4-6

Printed in the United States of America

For my wonderful big brother,
Stephen Lander, who lived twice the life
in half the time, and whose home was
filled with love and rescue dogs.

If you remember our Cooper
you will not be surprised to hear
he is now even more civilized.

While he's mostly quite polished,
he has one awful habit.

He won't ever listen once he sees a rabbit.

One day Cooper's uncle took him out in the yard,

but he didn't take the leash, thought it wouldn't be hard.

In a flash Cooper spied it, then ran off for the bunny.

Uncle Stephen yelled "COME! IT'S REALLY NOT FUNNY!"

Watching in awe as our mutt cleared the fence, we gasped at the bunny, and then it all just made sense.

Don't get me wrong, his intentions are kind.

It's making a buddy that he has on his mind.

One after the other they hightailed it through town.

Cooper couldn't understand, "Why won't that hare just slow down?"

8

Through playgrounds and parks, they galloped about,
and made a huge mess of the fifth grade cookout.

When they found themselves laughing at the
mayhem they made,
the rabbit then realized he need not be afraid.

Soon Cooper returned and the drama did end.

He came back with Jack Rabbit, his new furry friend.

Just as Cooper was found as a stray,

Jack had been lost and had nowhere to stay.

Cooper asked our parents if he could have his own pet.

He promised he'd make sure that his needs were all met.

13

With kindness and love they welcomed Jack in,
and connections were made where differences had been.

"An unlikely pair," the neighbors all say,
"A dog and a hare, so close in each way?"

It's no big deal that they aren't
the same. A bunny and hound?
A name is just a name.

15

Cooper and Jack are so much alike.
They love to explore, on foot or
by bike.

Playing inside or out, it depends on
the weather.
Either way, they have fun just
being together.

Museums and cafes, the movies and stores,
(though the hardest part is opening the doors.)

You'll find them in bookstores just
browsing the aisles, or golfing or sailing a
few nautical miles.

18

Playing tennis or chess,
hiking or drawing, or just
finding some sticks for some
old-fashioned gnawing.

When Jack is homesick for his old bunny friends.
He shares how he feels. He never pretends.

When either is feeling disappointed or blue,
the other is there to help him pull through.

With someone to talk with and be understood,
having a true pal to lean on is so very good.

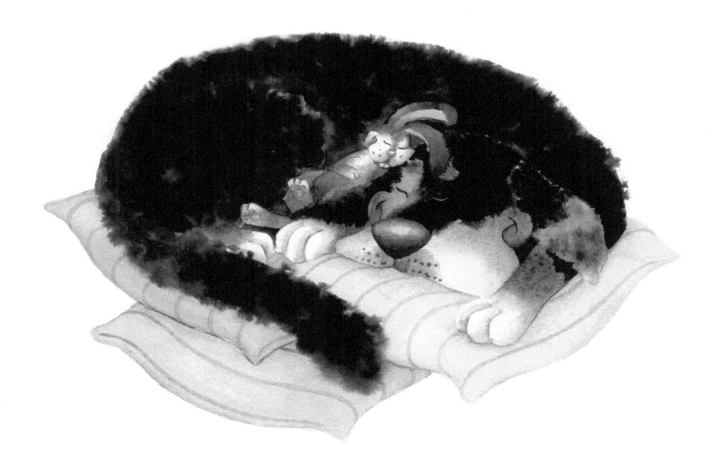

With friendship that's real being yourself should feel easy.

Sharing emotions with friends should never feel cheesy.

Sometimes when the day has gone horribly wrong,
they go to the garage and create a new song.

With Cooper on drums and Jack on guitar,
it's a sight, let's admit, it's a little bizarre.

As the kids enjoy dancing at the rockin' jam session, they realize they're learning a valuable lesson:

23

Keep your mind and heart open when you meet someone new.

You might find a great friend even if different from you!

The End

About the Author

Michelle Lander Feinberg is an attorney who lives in Massachusetts with her husband, Andrew, their five children, a dog, and a mouse. As a life-long animal advocate, she is a strong supporter of animal welfare organizations and does her best to spread the word of the importance of adopting pets from animal shelters and rescue groups. This is her second published children's book in the Cooper the Dog series.

About the Illustrator

Anna Mosca is an Italian illustrator. Currently, she is studying philosophy at the University of Genoa, plus art and illustration at the International School of Comics. She loves to give voice to characters, and make their fantasies come to life. Anna is an enthusiastic, humorous person full of creativity and determination. Her motto: "Head in the clouds but feet on the ground!"

Acknowledgments

I am sending my greatest appreciation to my editor, Robert Astle, of Highline Editorial, and my publisher, Lisa Akoury-Ross, of SDP Publishing Solutions, for all of your advice and for shepherding me through this entire process. Howard Johnson and Anna Mosca, your creativity and amazing artwork helped bring Cooper to life. Thank you. I am grateful to my loving husband, Andrew, and to our five fantastic children, for your love, support, and honest feedback.

Information on Pet Adoption

Pets can be a wonderful addition to the family. Today there are many homeless animals that are looking for families to love! If your family is ready for a new pet, you can help find the perfect match at a shelter! Looking for a specific breed? Almost all breeds have rescue groups dedicated to finding homes for their purebred homeless dogs. A great place to start online is a website that connects almost all of the shelters and rescue groups in one place, such as www.petfinder.com.

Please Don't Tell Cooper That Jack is a Rabbit

Michelle Lander Feinberg

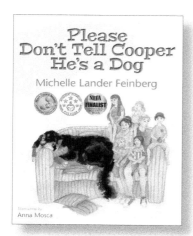

www.cooperthedog.com

Publisher: SDP Publishing

Also available in ebook format

Available at all major bookstores

Also by the author:

Please Don't Tell Cooper He's a Dog

CPSIA information can be obtained
at www.ICGtesting.com
Printed in the USA
LVHW072235151021
700403LV00012B/43

9 781736 199039